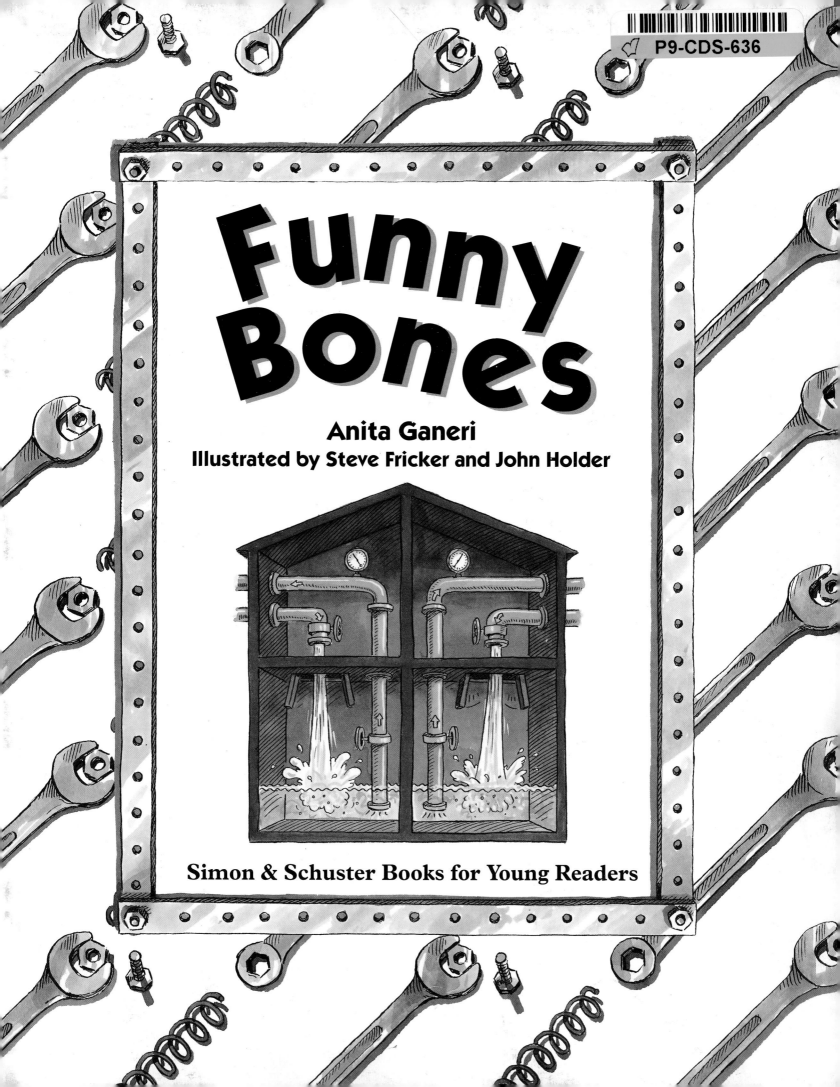

Funny Bones

Anita Ganeri

Illustrated by Steve Fricker and John Holder

Simon & Schuster Books for Young Readers

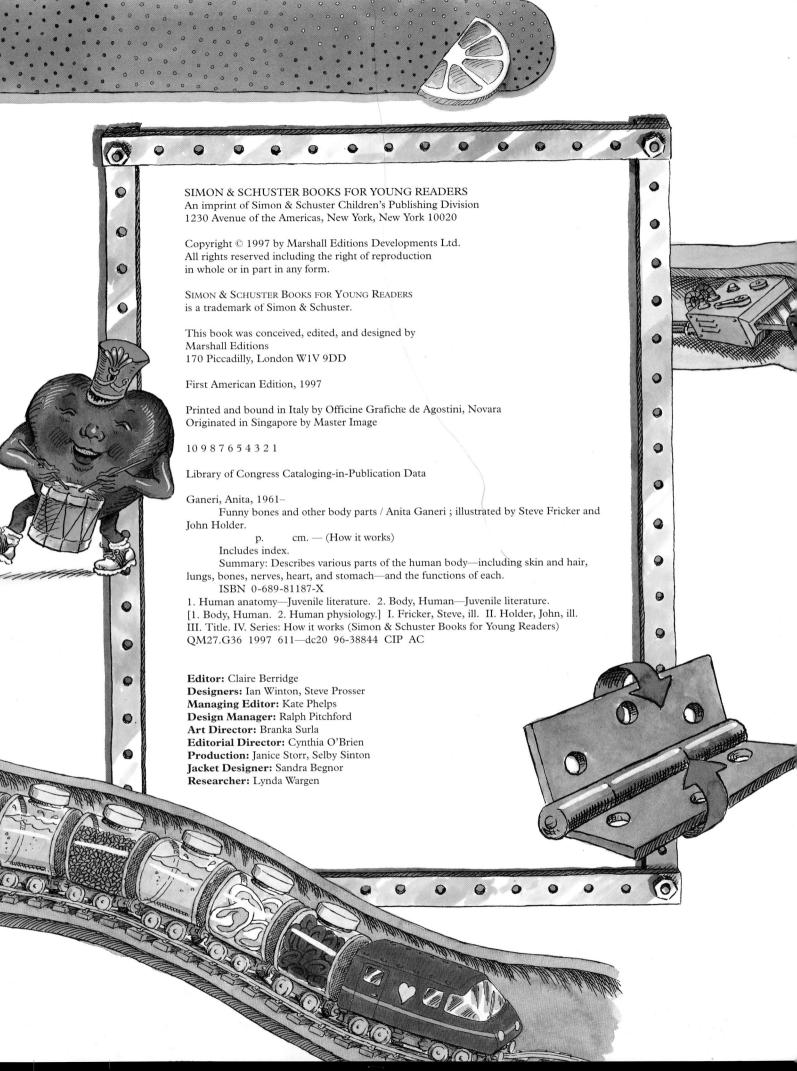

SIMON & SCHUSTER BOOKS FOR YOUNG READERS
An imprint of Simon & Schuster Children's Publishing Division
1230 Avenue of the Americas, New York, New York 10020

SIMON & SCHUSTER BOOKS FOR YOUNG READERS
is a trademark of Simon & Schuster.

This book was conceived, edited, and designed by
Marshall Editions
170 Piccadilly, London W1V 9DD

First American Edition, 1997

Printed and bound in Italy by Officine Grafiche de Agostini, Novara
Originated in Singapore by Master Image

10 9 8 7 6 5 4 3 2 1

Library of Congress Cataloging-in-Publication Data

Ganeri, Anita, 1961–
        Funny bones and other body parts / Anita Ganeri ; illustrated by Steve Fricker and
John Holder.
                p.   cm. — (How it works)
        Includes index.
        Summary: Describes various parts of the human body—including skin and hair,
lungs, bones, nerves, heart, and stomach—and the functions of each.
        ISBN 0-689-81187-X
1. Human anatomy—Juvenile literature. 2. Body, Human—Juvenile literature.
[1. Body, Human. 2. Human physiology.] I. Fricker, Steve, ill. II. Holder, John, ill.
III. Title. IV. Series: How it works (Simon & Schuster Books for Young Readers)
QM27.G36 1997 611—dc20 96-38844 CIP AC

Editor: Claire Berridge
Designers: Ian Winton, Steve Prosser
Managing Editor: Kate Phelps
Design Manager: Ralph Pitchford
Art Director: Branka Surla
Editorial Director: Cynthia O'Brien
Production: Janice Storr, Selby Sinton
Jacket Designer: Sandra Begnor
Researcher: Lynda Wargen

CONTENTS

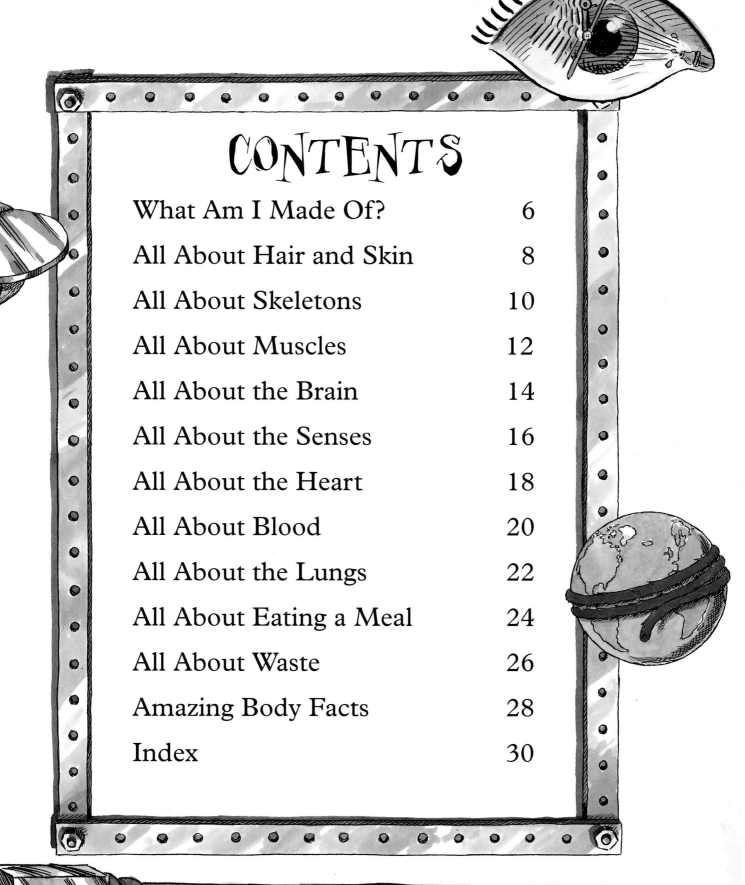

What Am I Made Of?	6
All About Hair and Skin	8
All About Skeletons	10
All About Muscles	12
All About the Brain	14
All About the Senses	16
All About the Heart	18
All About Blood	20
All About the Lungs	22
All About Eating a Meal	24
All About Waste	26
Amazing Body Facts	28
Index	30

Your body is truly amazing! Take a look in the mirror. What do you see? Eyes, hair, fingers, toes . . . And that's just on the outside. There are lots more body parts inside you, all working together like a well-oiled machine to keep you alive. Each of these parts is made of cells. On their own, most cells are too tiny to see. But put them together, and you've got *you*!

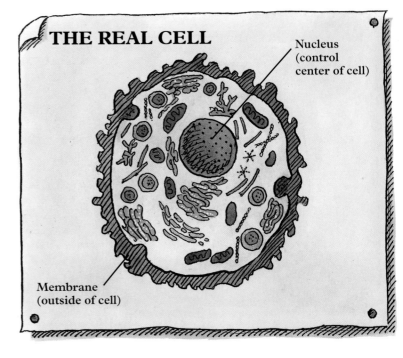

THE REAL CELL

Nucleus (control center of cell)

Membrane (outside of cell)

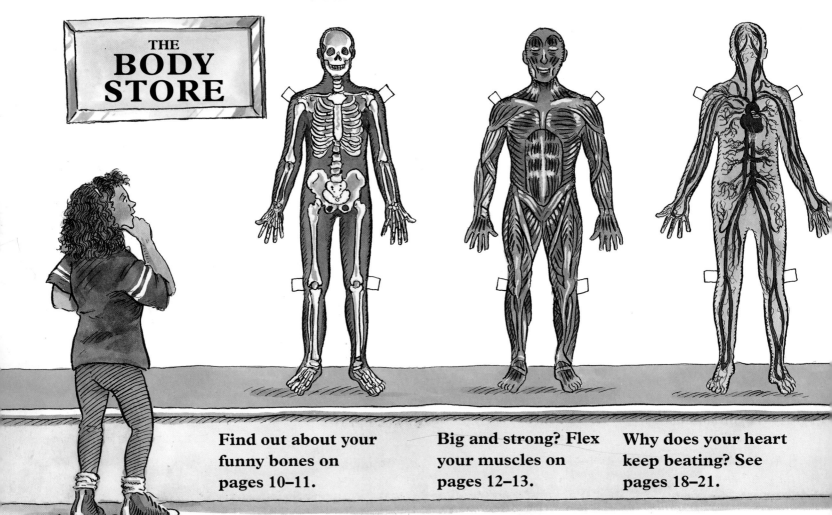

Skeleton

Muscles

Heart and blood

THE **BODY STORE**

Find out about your funny bones on pages 10–11.

Big and strong? Flex your muscles on pages 12–13.

Why does your heart keep beating? See pages 18–21.

BODY BUILDERS

Cells are the building blocks of your body. There are millions and millions of them, with different jobs to do. Some make your blood, bones, and skin. Others make your brain, muscles, and nerves. Cells can split into two, creating new ones that make you grow.

RECIPE FOR A BODY
206 bones
640 muscles
9 pints of blood
all-over skin
5 million hairs
10 toenails
10 fingernails
2 eyes
2 ears
1 nose
32 teeth
ORGANS: 1 heart; 1 liver; 1 stomach; 2 lungs; 2 kidneys; 1 spleen; 1 gallbladder; 1 pancreas; 2 intestines (1 large, 1 small)

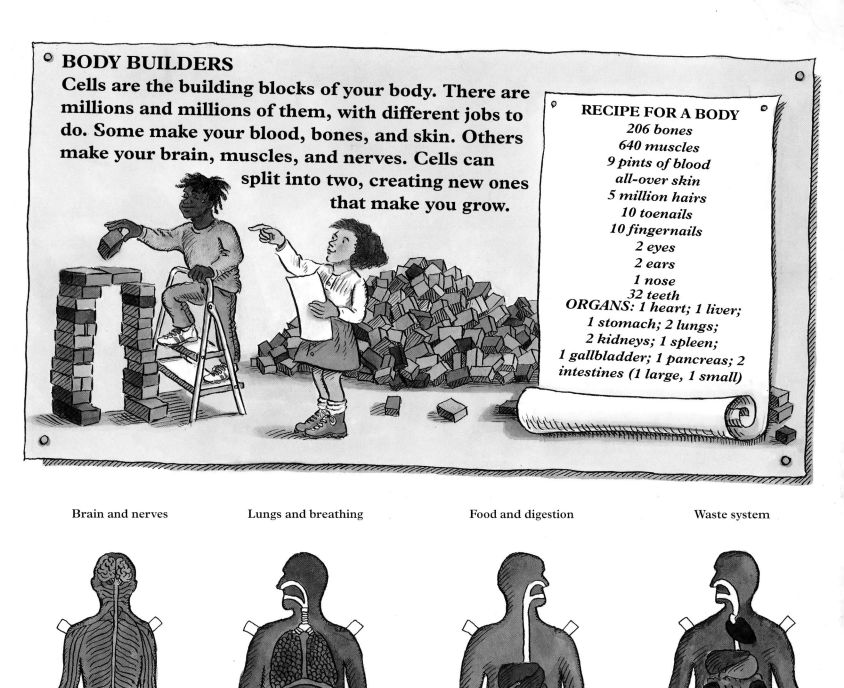

Brain and nerves

Lungs and breathing

Food and digestion

Waste system

Read all about your amazing brain on pages 14–15.

Breathe in. . . . learn about lungs on pages 22–23.

Where does your food go? Find out on pages 24–25.

What about the things you don't need? See pages 26–27.

Your whole body is covered in stretchy skin. Skin holds your body firmly together and protects your insides from harm. It helps you to touch and feel things. And it can mend itself if you cut it. That's not all! Growing out of your skin are your hair and nails. Hair keeps your head warm in the cold and keeps the sun off it. And nails are useful when you've got an itch. . . .

Like a diver's wet suit, skin is hard-wearing and waterproof. But it also lets you sweat on a hot day to cool you down. *Phew!*

Your skin makes oil to keep it soft and supple. Otherwise it would become wrinkly, like it does in the bath.

Hair

Freckle

Sweat

Epidermis (growing skin)

Sebaceous gland (oil-making gland)

Skin is made of cells that overlap like tiny roof tiles.

Dermis (second layer of skin)

OIL

Sweat gland

Hair follicle

Wavy hair follicle

Straight hair follicle

Curly hair follicle

HAIR STYLES
About five million hairs grow on your body. More than 100,000 of these are on the top of your head.

Hair grows out of tiny holes in your skin called follicles. The type of hair you've got depends on the shape of your follicles.

Wavy hair grows from oval follicles. Straight hair grows from round follicles. Curly hair grows from flat follicles.

THE REAL HAIR AND SKIN
Skin is made of two layers. The upper layer is the epidermis, the lower the dermis. The outside of the epidermis is made of dead skin cells. As these wear out, new cells from the bottom of the epidermis replace them. Your hair and nails are also made of dead cells. That's why it doesn't hurt when you cut them.

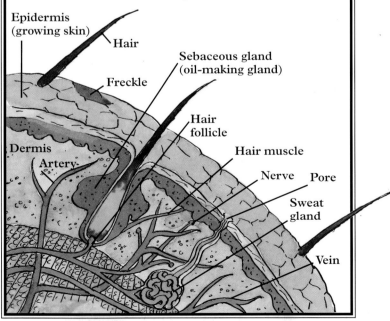

Epidermis (growing skin)

Hair

Sebaceous gland (oil-making gland)

Freckle

Hair follicle

Dermis

Artery

Hair muscle

Nerve

Pore

Sweat gland

Vein

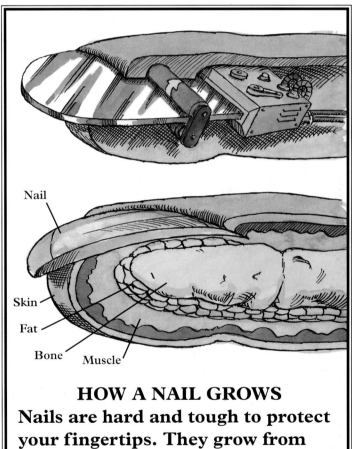

Nail

Skin

Fat

Bone

Muscle

HOW A NAIL GROWS
Nails are hard and tough to protect your fingertips. They grow from nail roots under the skin. Your fingernails grow faster than your toenails. And all your nails grow faster in summer than in winter!

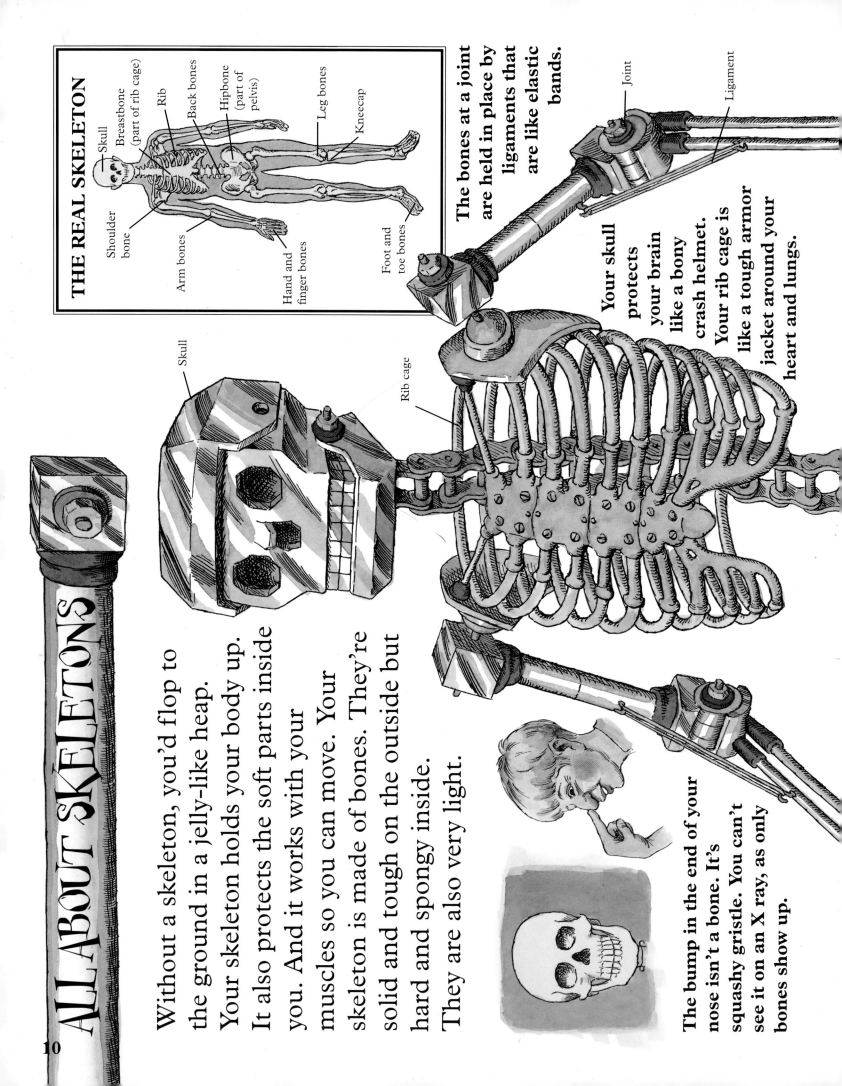

ALL ABOUT SKELETONS

Without a skeleton, you'd flop to the ground in a jelly-like heap. Your skeleton holds your body up. It also protects the soft parts inside you. And it works with your muscles so you can move. Your skeleton is made of bones. They're solid and tough on the outside but hard and spongy inside. They are also very light.

The bump in the end of your nose isn't a bone. It's squashy gristle. You can't see it on an X ray, as only bones show up.

THE REAL SKELETON

Skull
Breastbone (part of rib cage)
Rib
Back bones
Hipbone (part of pelvis)
Leg bones
Kneecap
Shoulder bone
Arm bones
Hand and finger bones
Foot and toe bones

The bones at a joint are held in place by ligaments that are like elastic bands.

Joint

Ligament

Your skull protects your brain like a bony crash helmet. Your rib cage is like a tough armor jacket around your heart and lungs.

Skull

Rib cage

Joints are places where two bones meet. You couldn't bend your arms or legs without them!

Hipbone (part of pelvis)

Your skeleton's like a gigantic jigsaw puzzle. Each bone needs to fit in its own proper place to make the whole skeleton work.

Femur bone

The smallest bone is the stirrup bone inside your ear.

It is only as long as a grain of rice (much smaller than shown here).

The longest, strongest bone is the femur bone in your thigh.

Anvil bone

Stirrup bone

More than half of your bones are in your hands and feet. They let you make small, quick movements.

HOW JOINTS WORK

Hinge joint

The joints in your elbows, knees, and fingers are like the hinges that open and close a door.

Ball-and-socket joint

Your shoulders and hips are called ball-and-socket joints. The ball rotates in the socket to move your arm or leg.

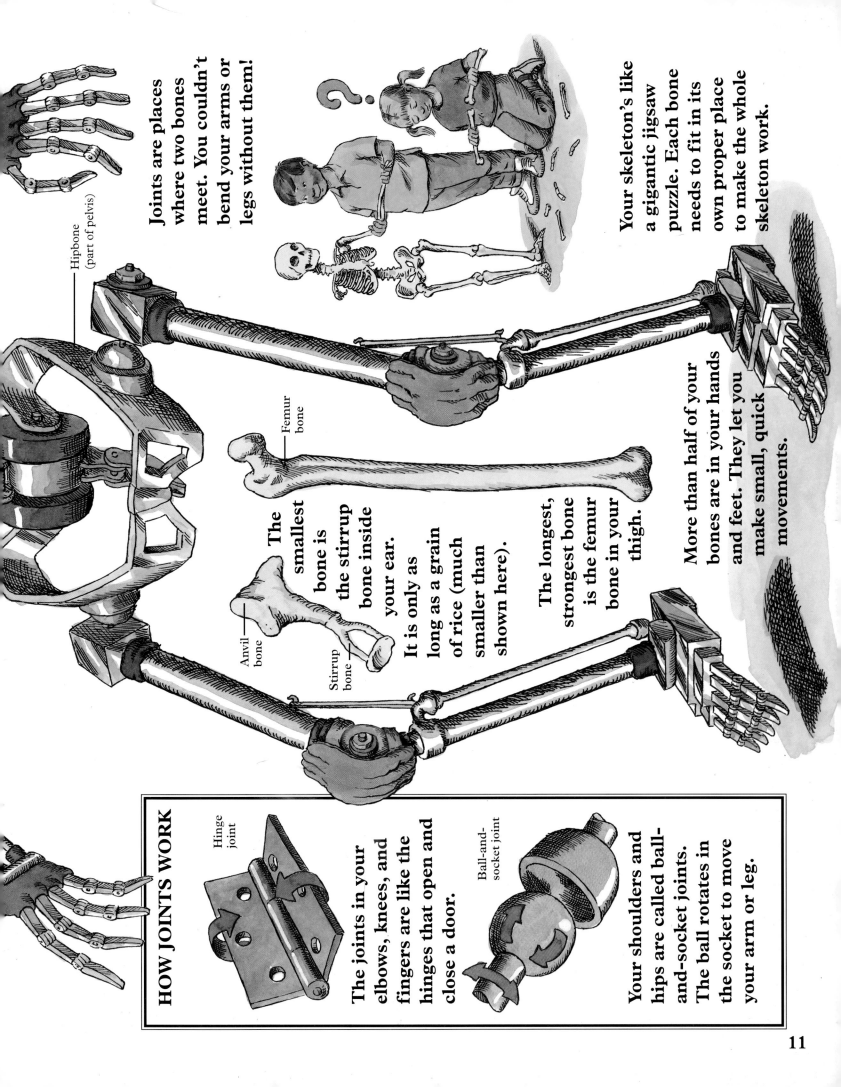

11

ALL ABOUT MUSCLES

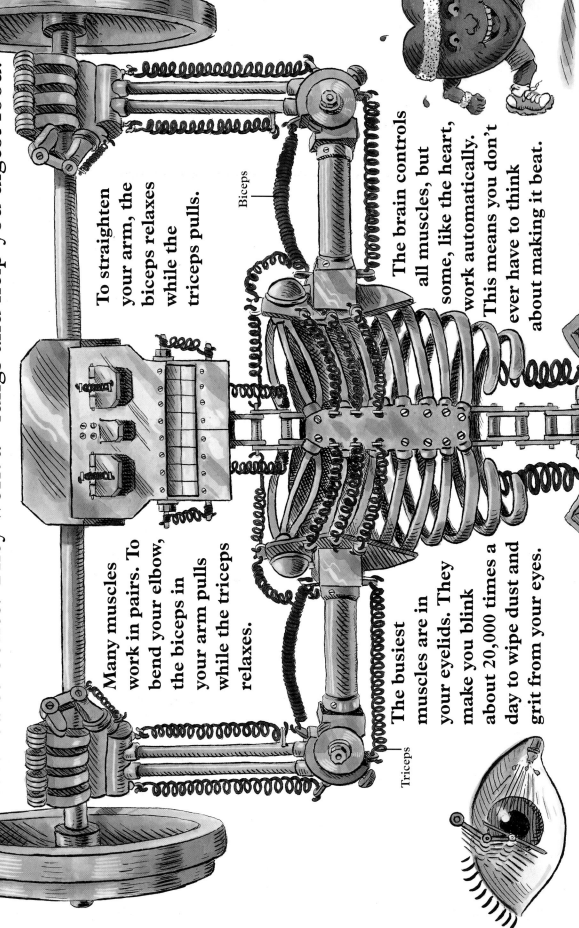

You might not be as strong as a weight lifter but you've got just as many muscles! Some are bit like springs, pulling on your bones to make you move. Other muscles work your heart and lungs and help you digest food. They work attached to bones.

To straighten your arm, the biceps relaxes while the triceps pulls.

Biceps

The brain controls all muscles, but some, like the heart, work automatically. This means you don't ever have to think about making it beat.

Many muscles work in pairs. To bend your elbow, the biceps in your arm pulls while the triceps relaxes.

The busiest muscles are in your eyelids. They make you blink about 20,000 times a day to wipe dust and grit from your eyes.

Triceps

THE REAL MUSCLES

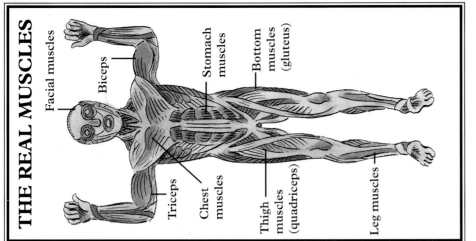

- Facial muscles
- Biceps
- Stomach muscles
- Bottom muscles (gluteus)
- Triceps
- Chest muscles
- Thigh muscles (quadriceps)
- Leg muscles

There are about 640 muscles all over your body, under your skin. They are made of bundles of tiny, thin fibers, like stretchy elastic threads. Each of these fibers is made of even finer threads. The whole muscle is covered with a stretchy layer to keep it in shape.

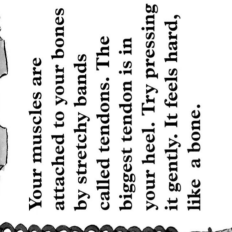

Your muscles are attached to your bones by stretchy bands called tendons. The biggest tendon is in your heel. Try pressing it gently. It feels hard, like a bone.

A third of your body weight is made up of muscle. Your biggest muscles are in your bottom! The smallest muscles are deep inside your ears.

Muscles need lots of energy to make them work. They get this from oxygen in the air you breathe and from the food you eat. Your blood carries the oxygen and food to your muscles.

MAKING A FACE

To make a face as ugly as this one, you use about thirty muscles! These don't pull on bones, like the muscles in your arms do. They pull on your skin instead.

Ouch!

Your brain is the most amazing machine! It's like a computer inside your head. Every bit of your body is controlled by your brain. It makes you move, think, feel, and remember. Your body sends information to your brain. Then your brilliant brain sorts it out and tells your body what to do. The messages whiz back and forth down long, thin wires called nerves. Parts of your brain work even when you're asleep, but at least some of it gets a rest!

When you stub your toe, pain signals race from your foot to your brain. *Ouch!* Your brain quickly tells you to pull your foot away.

SPEEDY NERVES

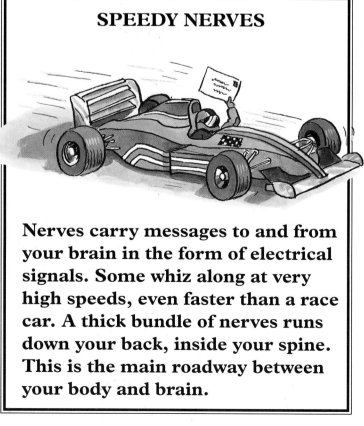

Nerves carry messages to and from your brain in the form of electrical signals. Some whiz along at very high speeds, even faster than a race car. A thick bundle of nerves runs down your back, inside your spine. This is the main roadway between your body and brain.

PLANNING

SPEECH

MATH SKILLS

DRAWING AND WRITING

TASTE

HEARTBEAT CONTROL

You need a good map to find your way around your brain! It's divided into different areas, each with its own job to do.

It does not matter how big or small your brain is, because size makes no difference to how smart you are! An adult's brain weighs about three pounds. It looks like a lump of soft gray cauliflower. *Yuck!*

THE REAL BRAIN

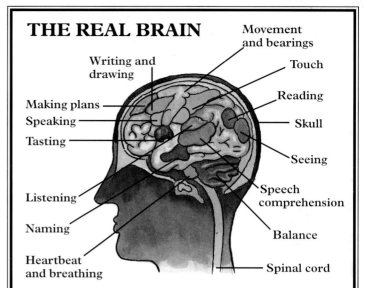

Movement and bearings
Writing and drawing
Touch
Making plans
Reading
Speaking
Skull
Tasting
Seeing
Speech comprehension
Listening
Naming
Balance
Heartbeat and breathing
Spinal cord

The main part of your brain is divided into two sides, left and right. If you're right-handed, it means the left side of your brain is in control. If you're left-handed, the right side is in charge.

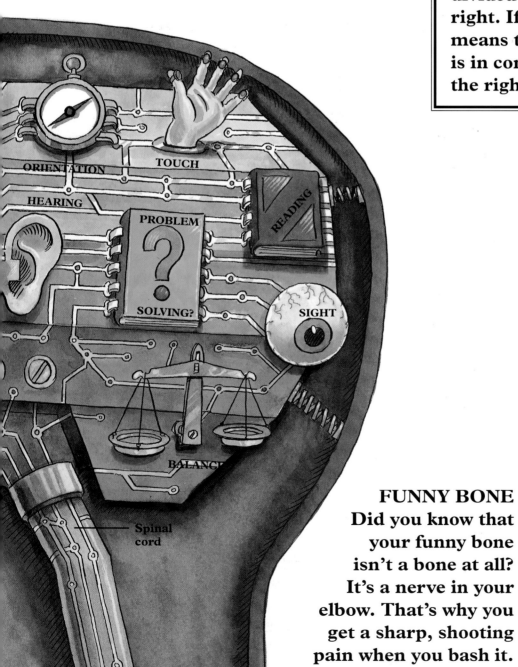

ORIENTATION
TOUCH
HEARING
READING
PROBLEM
?
SOLVING?
SIGHT
BALANCE
Spinal cord

THE REAL NERVOUS SYSTEM

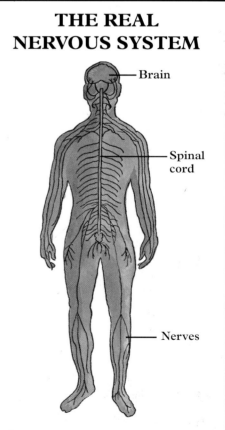

Brain
Spinal cord
Nerves

The nervous system is the pathway of nerves that run throughout your body carrying messages.

FUNNY BONE
Did you know that your funny bone isn't a bone at all? It's a nerve in your elbow. That's why you get a sharp, shooting pain when you bash it.

15

ALL ABOUT THE SENSES

How do you keep track of the world around you? By using your five senses, that's how! Your eyes see, your nose smells, your skin feels, your ears hear, and your tongue tastes. Each sense receiver is connected by nerves to your amazing brain.

You feel things with your skin. It tells you if things are hot or cold, rough or smooth. Your skin also feels pain. This warns your body of danger.

Eye

Nose

Hand

Bitter
Sour
Salt
Sweet

Thousands of tiny bumps cover your tongue. They are called taste buds. They tell you if things taste bitter, sour, sweet, or salty.

TASTE AND SMELL

Have you noticed how bland food tastes when you've got a cold? When you can't smell your food very well, you can't taste it very well either, because taste and smell work together.

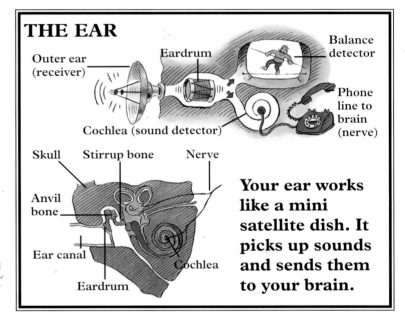

Ear

SEEING THE LIGHT!

Vitamin A, which is found in carrots and many other foods, helps the sensitive cells in your eyes pick up light. Luckily all ordinary diets supply enough Vitamin A to make sure you see properly.

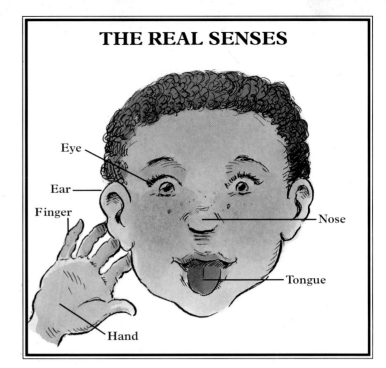

THE REAL SENSES

Eye

Ear

Finger

Nose

Tongue

Hand

THE EAR

Outer ear (receiver)

Eardrum

Balance detector

Cochlea (sound detector)

Phone line to brain (nerve)

Skull   Stirrup bone   Nerve

Anvil bone

Ear canal

Cochlea

Eardrum

Your ear works like a mini satellite dish. It picks up sounds and sends them to your brain.

THE EYE

Message to brain (nerve)

Light rays

Lens

Jelly (vitreous humor)

Screen (retina)

Cornea

Lens

Retina

Pupil

Vitreous humor

Optic nerve

Your eye works like a tiny camera. Light goes in through a hole at the front (the pupil). This light makes the picture you see.

FROM HEAD

TO HEAD

FROM BODY

TO BODY

TO LUNGS

Artery taking oxygen to the rest of the body

Vein bringing carbon dioxide to the heart

Artery taking carbon dioxide to the lungs

FROM LUNGS

Clench your fist tightly. Now it's about the same size as your heart. Its job is to pump blood throughout your body, all the time, day and night. This lets blood carry food and oxygen to all of your cells. Each pump of your heart is called a heartbeat.

Arteries take carbon dioxide from the heart to the lungs. Veins bring oxygen to the heart from the lungs.

RIGHT

LEFT

Vein bringing oxygen to the left side of the heart

Arteries are the blood vessels that take oxygen from the heart to the rest of the body.

Veins are the blood vessels that bring carbon dioxide to the heart from the rest of the body.

FROM LUNGS

Vein bringing oxygen to the left side of the heart

In the space of a heartbeat:
1. Stale blood from your body flows into the right side of your heart. Then it's pumped into your lungs.

2. In your lungs, your blood picks up more oxygen, which your body needs to stay alive.

3. Blood from your lungs flows into the left side of your heart. Then it's pumped to the rest of your body.

Right atrium

Left atrium

TO LUNGS

TO HEAD AND BODY

FROM HEAD AND BODY

FROM LUNGS

Right ventricle

Left ventricle

INSIDE YOUR HEART
Your heart is divided into four chambers, with walls of muscle in between. Thick pipes and tubes connect the two top chambers with the two chambers below.

WHERE IS YOUR HEART?
Your heart sits in the middle of your chest, slightly to the left, between your two lungs. It's made of strong muscle.

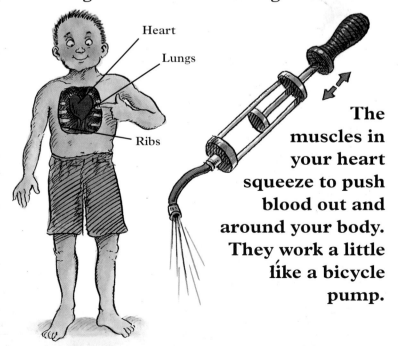

Heart

Lungs

Ribs

The muscles in your heart squeeze to push blood out and around your body. They work a little like a bicycle pump.

Hearts are often linked with love. People used to think you felt things with your heart, not with your brain.

Did you know that your heart beats about 100,000 times a day? That's almost seventy times a minute.

THE REAL HEART

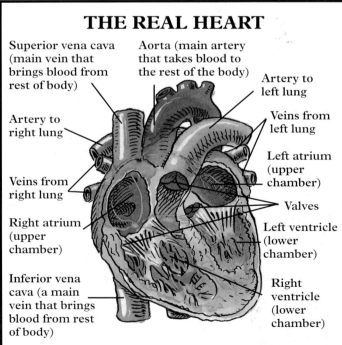

Superior vena cava (main vein that brings blood from rest of body)

Aorta (main artery that takes blood to the rest of the body)

Artery to left lung

Artery to right lung

Veins from left lung

Veins from right lung

Left atrium (upper chamber)

Right atrium (upper chamber)

Valves

Left ventricle (lower chamber)

Inferior vena cava (a main vein that brings blood from rest of body)

Right ventricle (lower chamber)

Flaps in your heart, called valves, let blood through but then snap shut to stop it from flowing backward again.

WASTE

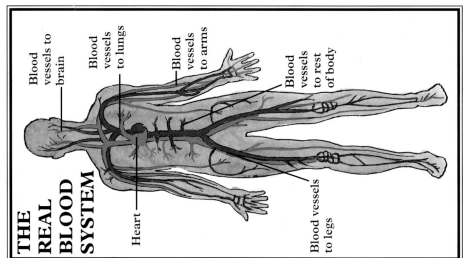

THE REAL BLOOD SYSTEM

Blood vessels to brain

Blood vessels to lungs

Blood vessels to arms

Blood vessels to rest of body

Heart

Blood vessels to legs

Blood flows around your body through tiny tubes called blood vessels. They're like subway tunnels, carrying trainloads of oxygen and food to nourish your body.

ALL ABOUT BLOOD

Together, your heart and blood make up your circulatory system. "Circulatory" means going around and around. It takes about a minute for a blood cell to travel all the way through the system.

HEART

LEFT LUNG

LEFT

RIGHT

RIGHT LUNG

What's the red sticky stuff that seeps out if you cut yourself? Your blood, that's what! You need it to stay alive. Blood carries oxygen from the air you breathe, plus useful things from the food you eat, to every single part of you. And it helps fight off germs that make you ill.

If all the tubes inside your body were put end to end, they'd go around the Earth two and a half times!

RED CELLS

Blood is made up of tiny cells floating in watery liquid (plasma). In just one drop of blood, there are more than two million red blood cells, 5,000 white blood cells, and 250,000 platelets (parts of cells).

Adults have about nine pints of blood flowing through their body. When you were born, you had less than two pints of blood in your body.

In the tubes carrying blood back to the heart, there are valves, like trapdoors. They stop your blood from flowing the wrong way.

RED CELLS

Red blood carries oxygen from your heart and lungs to the rest of your body. When the oxygen is used up, the blood turns a bluish color. Then it travels back to your heart and lungs for fresh supplies to start all over again.

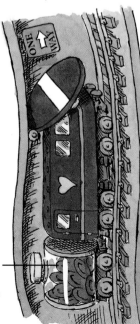

RED CELLS

WHITE CELLS

PLASMA

PLATELETS

WATER

FOOD

OXYGEN

WASTE

You probably take breathing for granted. This is because you breathe all the time, without having to think. It's automatic. Your cells need a gas called oxygen to make them work. You get this from the air you breathe. Your cells use this oxygen to get energy from the food you eat. As they do this, they make a waste gas, called carbon dioxide. This is the stale air that you breathe out. The main parts of your body used for breathing are your two lungs.

Fully grown lungs can hold an amazing nine pints of air.

When you breathe in, air goes down into your lungs. Your chest expands so your lungs have room to fill with air.

AIR IN

Windpipe

Vocal cords

Lungs

Ribs push outward

Rib

Diaphragm flattens.

SPEAK UP!

Your vocal cords are two thin strings stretched over your throat. When you speak, air flows across them and makes them wobble. This wobbling produces the sound of your voice.

Each lung has millions of tiny air sacs. These are covered in blood vessels that take oxygen from the air you breathe in and bring carbon dioxide that you breathe out.

Blood vessels

Alveoli (air sacs)

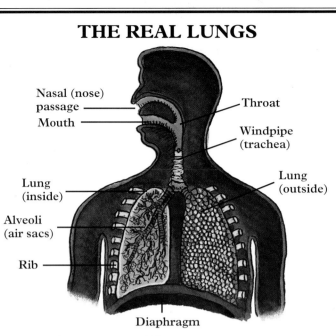

THE REAL LUNGS

Nasal (nose) passage

Mouth

Throat

Windpipe (trachea)

Lung (inside)

Lung (outside)

Alveoli (air sacs)

Rib

Diaphragm

Your lungs are like two spongy bags in your chest. Together with your mouth, nose, and throat, they make up your body's respiratory system. "Respiratory" means "breathing."

AIR OUT

Windpipe

Vocal cords

When you breathe out, your ribs push down and air is squeezed out of your lungs and up through your throat. Your diaphragm, a sheet of muscle under your lungs, moves upward.

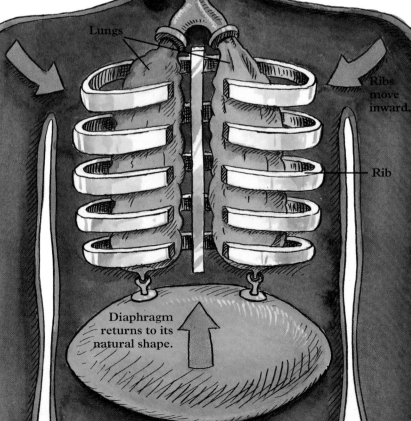

Lungs

Ribs move inward.

Rib

Diaphragm returns to its natural shape.

Hic! Hic! Do you ever get hiccups? *Hic!* They happen if your diaphragm twitches sharply and your vocal cords snap shut with a loud noise. Drinking out of the wrong side of a glass is just one of the cures you can try.

23

ALL ABOUT EATING A MEAL

Feeling hungry? That's your brain's way of telling you that your energy supplies are running low. Energy comes from food. First, food has to be broken down into tiny pieces that are absorbed into the blood. Your blood then carries the goodness from the food to your cells.

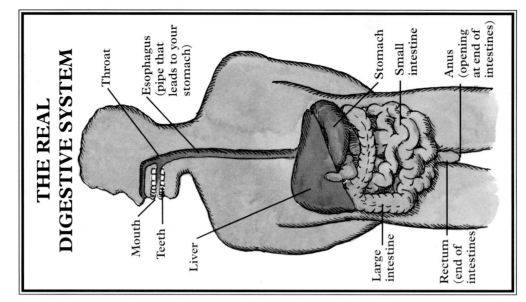

THE REAL DIGESTIVE SYSTEM

Throat

Esophagus (pipe that leads to your stomach)

Stomach

Small intestine

Anus (opening at end of intestines)

Mouth

Teeth

Liver

Large intestine

Rectum (end of intestines)

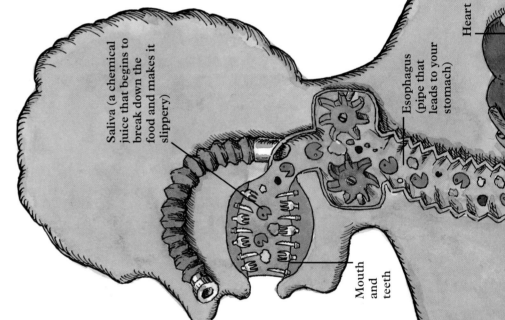

Saliva (a chemical juice that begins to break down the food and makes it slippery)

Esophagus (pipe that leads to your stomach)

Heart

Mouth and teeth

REAL TEETH

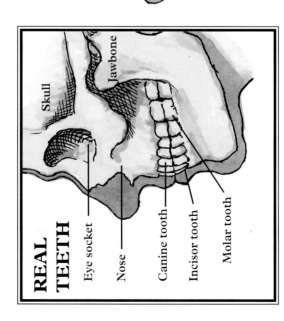

Skull

Jawbone

Eye socket

Nose

Canine tooth

Incisor tooth

Molar tooth

In your mouth, your teeth chop and chew your food. A coating of watery spit (saliva) makes food slippery and easy to swallow.

Next step . . . swallowing! When you swallow, the food slips down a long tube in your throat and into your stomach. *Gulp!*

In your stomach, the food is mashed and mushed into a slimy "soup." Special juices help to dissolve it. Your stomach's made of strong muscle. It stretches as it fills with food. Then the "soup" trickles down into another long tube.

The sides of the intestine tubes are made of strong muscles. They squeeze to push the food along them. It's a little like squeezing toothpaste out a tube when you brush your teeth.

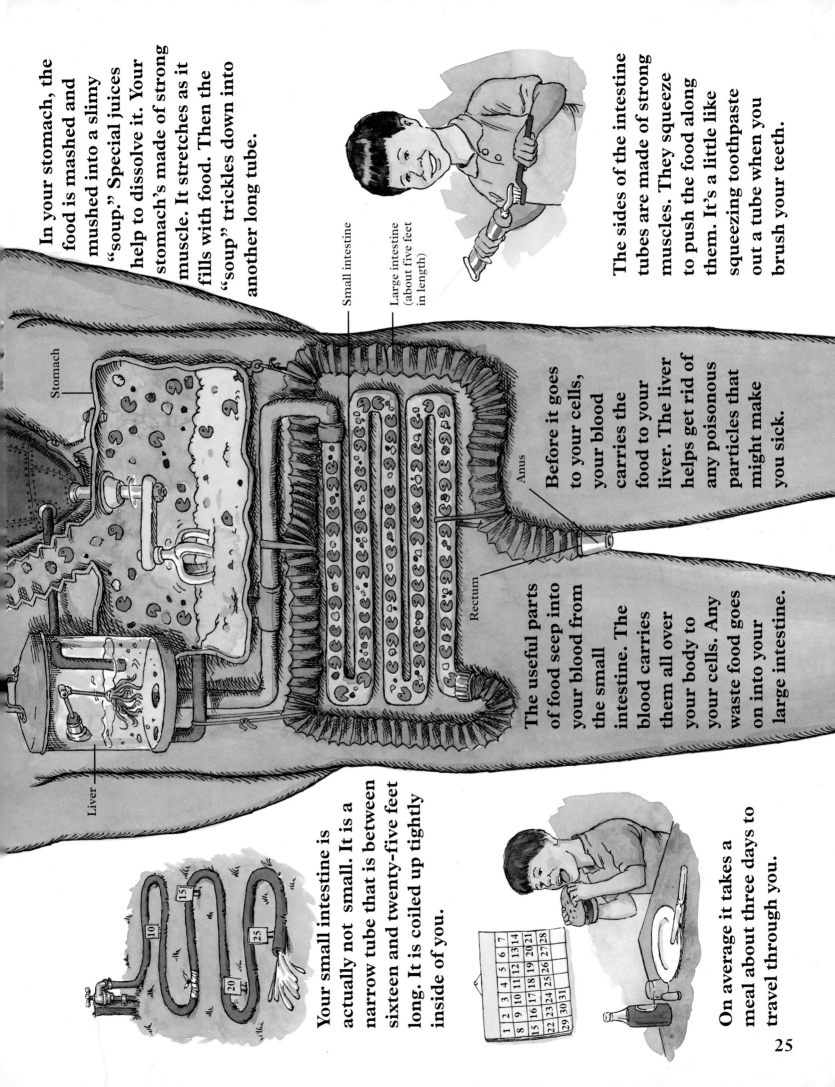

Stomach

Liver

Small intestine

Large intestine (about five feet in length)

Anus

Rectum

Before it goes to your cells, your blood carries the food to your liver. The liver helps get rid of any poisonous particles that might make you sick.

The useful parts of food seep into your blood from the small intestine. The blood carries them all over your body to your cells. Any waste food goes on into your large intestine.

Your small intestine is actually not small. It is a narrow tube that is between sixteen and twenty-five feet long. It is coiled up tightly inside of you.

On average it takes a meal about three days to travel through you.

ALL ABOUT WASTE

Some parts of food cannot be used. If they stayed in your body, they'd poison your cells and make you sick. So your body gets rid of them as waste. When you go to the bathroom to urinate, you get rid of waste fluids and any dirty particles from your blood. When you have a bowel movement, you get rid of waste food.

Feeling sick? Vomiting is your body's way of getting rid of food that would otherwise make you sick. But you might also feel bad if you've eaten too much!

THE REAL WASTE SYSTEM

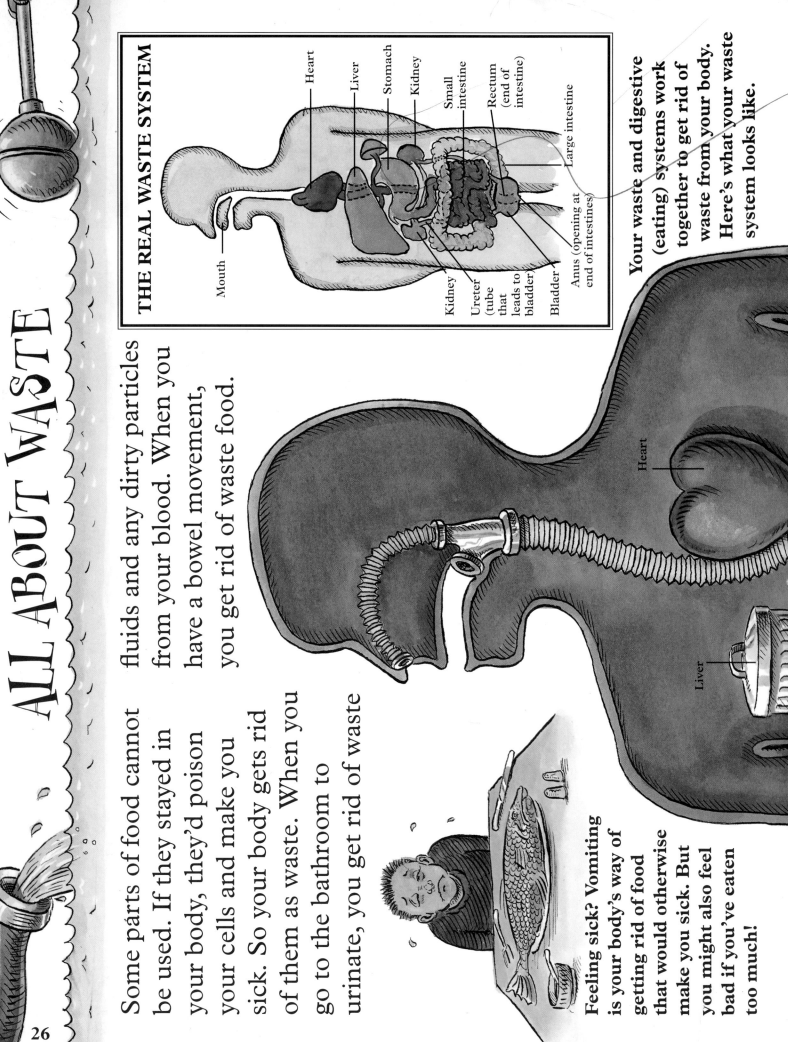

Heart
Liver
Stomach
Kidney
Small intestine
Rectum (end of intestine)
Large intestine
Mouth
Kidney
Ureter (tube that leads to bladder)
Bladder
Anus (opening at end of intestines)

Your waste and digestive (eating) systems work together to get rid of waste from your body. Here's what your waste system looks like.

Heart

Liver

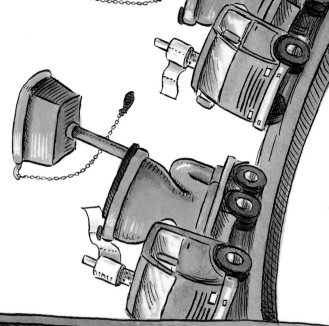

Your bladder is a small bag of muscle that stretches as it fills with urine. A ring of muscle around the neck stops the urine from seeping out. When you go to the bathroom, the muscle relaxes and lets the urine flow out along another tube.

Stomach

Kidney

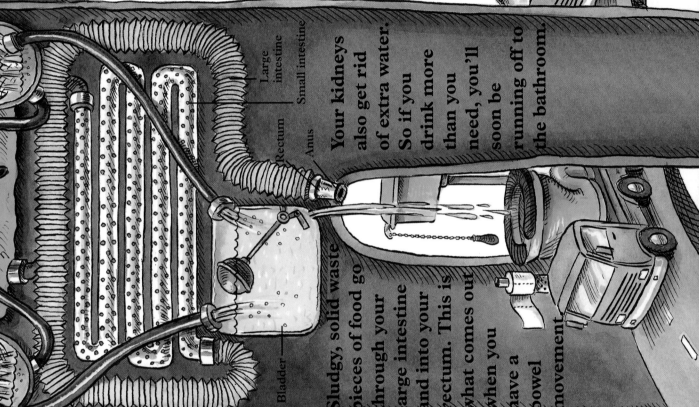

Large intestine

Small intestine

Rectum

Anus

Bladder

Kidney

Your kidneys also get rid of extra water. So if you drink more than you need, you'll soon be running off to the bathroom.

Sludgy, solid waste pieces of food go through your large intestine and into your rectum. This is what comes out when you have a bowel movement

Your liver works to clean the poisons from your digested food. It also takes some of the goodness from food and stores it until your body needs it.

THE REAL KIDNEY

Ureter (pipe that leads to the bladder)

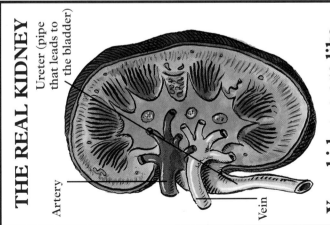

Artery

Vein

Your kidneys are like sieves. They take out the waste products from your blood. This liquid waste is called urine. It goes from the kidneys into your bladder.

AMAZING BODY FACTS

Welcome to the amazing world of the human body. At first glance, this might look like just an ordinary, everyday house. But take a closer look . . . it's full of astonishing facts and records about things your body can do.

Did you know that you grow in your sleep?

What color are these apples? About one in twenty people are red-green color-blind. This means that they can't tell the difference between red and green.

In your lifetime, you will eat and digest about thirty tons of food.

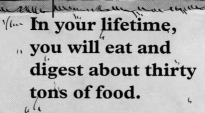

A man from India named Shridhar Chillal grew the longest fingernails in the world. Each nail on his left hand measured more than three feet.

Are you double-jointed? This doesn't mean you've got extra joints but that your ligaments are extra-stretchy.

The aorta is the body's biggest artery. It's nearly an inch wide—that's wider than your thumb.

Aorta 1 inch wide

The first heart transplant took place in 1967. Today surgeons can give people new lungs, kidneys, livers, skin, and blood.

In your life you will pass about 10,500 gallons of urine. That's around 500 bathtubs full!

500

Different people have different types of blood, called A, B, O, or AB.

Some cells live longer than others. Your brain cells have to last a lifetime. But red blood cells live only for four months.

Your skin is thinnest on your eyelids (.02 inches), and thickest on the soles of your feet (.2 inches or more).

HAPPY BIRTHDAY
Bone Cells
30 YEARS
Taste Cells
7 DAYS
Skin Cells
3 WEEKS

The strongest muscles are on each side of your mouth. You use them to bite with.

The sartorius is the longest muscle. It runs from your hip down to just below your knee. Its name is Latin for "tailor."

29

INDEX

air 22, 23
anus 24, 25, 26, 27
arteries 18, 19
    aorta 19, 29

bladder 26, 27
blood 6, 7, 13, 18, 19,
    20–21, 24, 25, 29
bones 6, 7, 10, 11,
    12, 13, 17
brain 7, 10, 12,
    14–15, 16, 17, 24
breathing 7, 22, 23

carbon dioxide 18,
    22, 23
cells 6, 7, 8, 18, 22,
    24, 25, 29
    blood cells 21
    membrane 6
    nucleus 6
circulatory system 20

diaphragm 22, 23
digestion 7, 26, 28
digestive system 26

ears 7, 11, 13, 16, 17
eating 24–25, 28
esophagus 24
eyes 7, 12, 16, 17,
    28, 29

food 7, 12, 13, 18,
    20, 21, 22, 24, 25,
    26, 27

hair 7, 8–9
    follicle 8, 9
heart 6, 7, 10, 12,
    18-19, 20, 21, 29
    chambers 19

intestines
    large 7, 24, 25, 26,
        27
    small 7, 24, 25, 26,
        27

joint 10, 11, 28

kidneys 7, 26, 27
    ureter 26, 27
knee 10, 11

ligament 10, 28
liver 7, 24, 25, 26, 27
lungs 7, 10, 18, 19,
    20, 21, 22–23
    alveoli 23

muscles 6, 7, 10,
    12–13, 19, 29
    biceps 12, 13
    quadriceps 13
    sartorius 29
    triceps 12, 13

nails 7, 8, 9, 28
nerves 7, 14, 15, 16,
    17
nervous system 15
nose 7, 10, 16, 17

oxygen 13, 18, 20, 21,
    22, 23

rectum 24, 25, 26, 27
respiratory system 23
ribs 10, 22, 23

saliva 24
sebaceous gland 8, 9
senses 16–17
skeleton 6, 10–11
skin 7–8, 13, 16, 29
    dermis 8, 9
    epidermis 8, 9
    pore 9
skull 10
sleep 14, 28
smell 16, 17
spinal cord 15
stomach 7, 24, 25,
    26, 27
sweat gland 8, 9

taste 16, 17
taste buds 16
teeth 7, 24
tendons 13
tongue 16, 17
touch 8

urine 26, 27, 29

valves 19, 21
veins 18, 19
    inferior vena cava
        19
    superior vena cava
        19
vocal cords 22, 23

waste 7, 21, 26–27
windpipe 22, 23